First edition 2016

Library of Congress Catalog Card Number pending
ISBN 978-0-7636-7312-3

16 17 18 19 20 21 CCP
1 2 3 4 5 6 7 8 9 10

Printed in Shenzhen, Guangdong, China

MIX
Paper from
responsible sources
FSC
www.fsc.org   FSC® C008047

This book was typeset in Maiandra.
The illustrations were done in watercolor and aquarelle pencil.

Candlewick Press
99 Dover Street
Somerville, Massachusetts 02144

visit us at www.candlewick.com

FIONA'S LITTLE LIE

ROSEMARY WELLS

CANDLEWICK PRESS

Fiona wanted to be Felix's Birthday Elf so much
she nearly fell off her chair.

"I'm the one!" shouted Fiona.

"You're the one!" said Felix.

Miss B wrote a note for Fiona's mama. The note was about baking birthday cupcakes for Felix's party.

Dear Fiona's Mama,

Fiona is Felix's Birthday Elf tomorrow.

Please help her bake birthday cupcakes for our class, and bring them in the morning!

Yours truly,
Miss B

Going home from school, Felix told his mama about Fiona being his Birthday Elf.

"She knows that I love vanilla cupcakes," said Felix, "with raspberry icing and lemon sprills!"

Meanwhile, on her way home from school, Fiona spotted a really sensational caterpillar.

POOF! went her Birthday Elf memory.

Miss B's note fluttered away, forgotten.

The next morning, Fiona skipped into
school empty-handed.

Just then Felix arrived in his new birthday shirt
and birthday pants.

"*Oh, no!*" Fiona squeaked. "*Oh, no!*"

But Felix was already in a cupcake trance.

Fiona could not bear to break her best
friend's heart.

"Your birthday cupcakes were stolen!"
Fiona said.

Felix gasped. "Do you think we could get
them back?" he asked.

"Oh, it's too late," said Fiona.

"The thieves just snatched them and snarfed
them down, every last one!"

Fiona could hear Felix's heart sink.

"There was nothing I could do!" she said. "There
were three of them and just one little me!"

"Thieves!" said Miss B. "Snarfing!"

"They gobbled them up like vampires!" said Fiona.
"They made horrifying gobbling noises!"

"Who would be so greedy?" asked Miss B.

Fiona took a deep breath. "Minkie, Dimples, and Bucky," she said. "That's who!"

Everyone knew the second-grade Terrible Three.

Miss B ran up to Mr. Bumpershock's second-grade classroom.

"I dreamed a cupcake dream last night," said Felix. "I could even smell the lemony sprills."

Fiona lay down on a yoga mat.

Something told Felix that Fiona was
on the edge of trouble.

Moments later, Minkie, Bucky, and Dimples
shuffled into the room.

"Are these the cupcake thieves?" asked
Mr. Bumpershock.

Fiona's whole body turned to stone.

Felix took Fiona's hand and whispered something in her ear.

"No!" answered Fiona. "It was *alligator* thieves who stole the cupcakes! Alligators named Dimples, Bucky, and Minkie!"

"Let's have the truth, please, Fiona," said Miss B.
"Truth and a good *I'm sorry* always clear the air."

Fiona could hear Felix breathing behind her.

Fiona whispered, "I forgot all about being a
Birthday Elf."

Fiona had to apologize to Felix, to Miss B, and to the Terrible Three.

"We'll have to celebrate with Birthday Bran Bars instead of cupcakes," said Miss B.

Suddenly they heard a voice in the hall.

It was Fiona's mama.

"I found the cupcake note on the floor of the car," she said, "and I baked extra!"

Everyone sang "Happy Birthday" to Felix.

The Terrible Three sang the loudest.

When they sang, they sounded just like
alligators croaking in the swamp.

Felix told Fiona she didn't have to listen.